Samuel French Acting

MW00461515

Marian, or The True Tale of Robin Hood

by Adam Szymkowicz

SAMUELFRENCH.COM   SAMUELFRENCH.CO.UK

FOR PRODUCTION ENQUIRIES

UNITED STATES AND CANADA
Info@SamuelFrench.com
1-866-598-8449

UNITED KINGDOM AND EUROPE
Plays@SamuelFrench.co.uk
020-7255-4302

Each title is subject to availability from Samuel French, depending upon country of performance. Please be aware that *MARIAN, OR THE TRUE TALE OF ROBIN HOOD* may not be licensed by Samuel French in your territory. Professional and amateur producers should contact the nearest Samuel French office or licensing partner to verify availability.

MUSIC USE NOTE

Licensees are solely responsible for obtaining formal written permission from copyright owners to use copyrighted music in the performance of this play and are strongly cautioned to do so. If no such permission is obtained by the licensee, then the licensee must use only original music that the licensee owns and controls. Licensees are solely responsible and liable for all music clearances and shall indemnify the copyright owners of the play(s) and their licensing agent, Samuel French, against any costs, expenses, losses and liabilities arising from the use of music by licensees. Please contact the appropriate music licensing authority in your territory for the rights to any incidental music.

IMPORTANT BILLING AND CREDIT REQUIREMENTS

If you have obtained performance rights to this title, please refer to your licensing agreement for important billing and credit requirements.

MARIAN, OR THE TRUE TALE OF ROBIN HOOD was originally commissioned by Flux Theatre Ensemble, with support from the Dramatists Guild Fund. It was developed in the Dorothy Strelsin New American Writer's Group at Primary Stages. It was produced from January 28 through February 11, 2017 at the New Ohio Theatre in New York by Flux Theatre Ensemble. The production was directed by Kelly O'Donnell, with scenic design by Will Lowry, lighting design by Jessica Greenberg, costume design by Izzy Fields, and sound design by Jacob Subotnick. The Production Stage Manager was Jodi M. Witherell. The cast was as follows:

ALANNA DALE	Jessica Angleskhan
MUCH THE MILLER'S SON	C. Bain
MARIAN/ROBIN	Becky Byers
TOMMY OF NO CONSEQUENCE	Alexandra Curran
SIR LENNY THE OBSERVANT / TANNER / GUARD	Aaron Parker Fouhey
PRINCE JOHN	Kevin R. Free
LITTLE JOHN	Jack Horton Gilbert
SHERIFF OF NOTTINGHAM / FRIAR TUCK	Mike Mihm
LADY SHIRLEY	Nandita Shenoy
LUCY / GUARD	Marnie Schulenburg
WILL SCARLETT	T. Thompson
SIR THEO THE PUNCTUAL / GUARD	Matthew Trumbull

Additional crew credits:
Technical Director, John Sochocky; Production Manager, Heather Cohn; Press Rep, August Schulenburg; Photography and graphic design by Isaiah Tanenbaum; Postcard illustration by Kristy Caldwell; Assistant Lighting Designer, Sienna Gonzalez and William Peterson; Fight Assistant, Stephen R. Scheide; Scenic Design Assistant, Lauren Girouard; Interns, Ashley Sohne and Emily Wilke

Special thanks in no particular order: Flux Theatre Ensemble for commissioning me to write this play and to the amazing cast and crew Flux assembled. The Primary Stages writing group, Michelle Bossy, Bennington College and the lovely students there who read it out loud for me the first time, Marsha Norman, David Lindsay-Abaire, Madhuri Shekar, Ted Malawer, Tearrance Arvelle Chisholm, Jonathan Payne, James Tyler, Jessica Moss, Martyna Majok, Krista Knight, Jenny Rachel Weiner, Dan McCabe. Kelly O'Donnell, August Schulenburg, Heather Cohn, The Dramatists Guild Fund, John and Rhoda Szymkowicz, Seth Glewen, Tish Dace, The Juilliard School, Kristen Palmer, and the many Robin Hoods that have come before as well as those who will come after.

CHARACTERS

MARIAN/ROBIN – Female

ALANNA DALE – Female

SHERIFF OF NOTTINGHAM – Male

LITTLE JOHN – Male, large

LADY SHIRLEY – Female

PRINCE JOHN – Male

TANNER – Any gender (can be doubled by actor who plays Theo or Lucy)

WILL SCARLETT – Female (played as male)

MUCH THE MILLER'S SON – Nonbinary (can be played by female, male, transgender, genderqueer, or nonbinary individual)

FRIAR TUCK – Male (in smaller cast, can be played by the same actor who plays the Sheriff)

TOMMY OF NO CONSEQUENCE – Played as male by any gender

SIR THEO THE PUNCTUAL – Played as male by any gender

SIR LENNY THE OBSERVANT – Played as male by any gender

LUCY – Played as female (can be doubled as Sir Lenny or a Guard)

GUARDS – Played as male by any gender (as many or as few as you like – up to fifteen speaking parts). In a smaller cast, Guard 1 and Guard 2 are played by Theo and Lenny. In a larger cast, each time Guard 1 and 2 appear, they can be played by different actors. The actor who plays Tommy can play a Guard toward the end, too. Same for the actor who plays Shirley.

NOTE: All parts are race non-specific. Marian/Robin need not be white. When women are playing men, fake moustaches and beards are probably a good idea. Try very hard to have a diverse cast. Almost forty percent of the U.S. is non-white. Can at least forty percent of your cast be? It would also be very helpful to have transgender, genderqueer, and/or nonbinary people involved in the production. Preferably more than one. The designations of female and male above can be used more as a guideline in the casting of this play. It would be great if Much was cast with a transgender, genderqueer, or nonbinary actor, but there are other parts that might be cast that way, too.

SETTING

England. Nottingham, Sherwood Forest. There is a modern-American bent to the play in terms of the themes and concerns of the characters. To that end, the English accents need not be particularly good. Design-wise, it may want to feel old, however, to make the contrast all the clearer.

Settings can be very simply implied. Keep it spare, flexible. Maybe this play should be done in a park or in the woods or in a castle.

TIME

During the Third Crusade. The 1190s.

For August Schulenburg,
a terrific writer and a wonderful person

1

The Castle Grounds

(*At rise, stage right, a row of archers facing the audience.* **ALANNA DALE**, *then* **MARIAN/ROBIN**, *wearing an old man's beard, then the* **SHERIFF**. *More archers are possible. It's probably best if the arrows are invisible/imaginary instead of having the archers shoot arrows into the audience. Behind the archers, the* **MERRY MEN** *in disguise, watching, and maybe a couple of the* **GUARDS**. *Stage left, perhaps on a platform,* **PRINCE JOHN** *is seated, with* **GUARDS** *guarding him.* **LADY SHIRLEY** *is seated nearby. Everyone is cheering on the archers, who are concentrating. It is very loud. All archers pull back in unison. The sounds of arrows going in. A hush, and then cheering. Then silence. All freeze.* **ALANNA** *steps forward, not frozen.*)

ALANNA. Some mornings, like this morning, I practice faces I might make during the day. Surprise. (*She makes a face.*) Concern. (*She makes a face.*) Respectful disagreement. (*She makes a face.*) This face means I'm going to be the first woman ever to win the royal archery tournament. (*She makes a face.*) This face means I'm the only one allowed to speak to the audience. (*She makes a face.*) Hi. I'm Alanna Dale. I'm a lady-in-waiting. And an archer. Welcome to Nottingham. It's very pretty, isn't it? If you don't pay too much attention to the filth. Or the smells. Or the rats. I'm in this story, but I also know things that I don't yet know in the story. Like for example, the old man beside me is actually Robin Hood. But I don't know that yet.

(All unfreeze. **LITTLE JOHN** *sidles up to* **MARIAN/ ROBIN**, *who is disguised as an old man.)*

LITTLE JOHN. Robin!

ROBIN. Don't say my name, Little John. I'm in disguise.

LITTLE JOHN. Sorry. Sorry. So, all is a go.

ROBIN. Excellent.

LITTLE JOHN. For the heist I mean.

ROBIN. I understand.

LITTLE JOHN. Of the contents of Prince John's vaults in Nottingham Castle.

ROBIN. Got it. Let's be a little more discreet, okay?

LITTLE JOHN. No problem. Discreee-shion is something I am good at.

ROBIN. Good. And don't stand next to me. You kind of stand out. Because of your size.

LITTLE JOHN. I'm trying to hunch over.

ROBIN. And you're doing splendid.

LITTLE JOHN. Okay, I'm going to go back over and work some more on the heisting. I'm very excited we're doing this, Robin.

ROBIN. Me too, old friend.

LITTLE JOHN. Robbing from the rich to give to the poor. It's like exactly what we're about.

ROBIN. That is true.

LITTLE JOHN. Because the poor have it rough.

ROBIN. They do.

LITTLE JOHN. And the taxes are so high! So very high!!

ROBIN. Okay. Let's be a little quieter.

LITTLE JOHN. Not to mention the disappearings. What happens, you think to the people who can't pay their taxes? Jail? Death? We should find out, Robin!

ROBIN. I know. Let's you concentrate on the heist right now and I'll concentrate on the archery. But yes, we will help.

LITTLE JOHN. We're helpful.

ROBIN. We try to be.

LITTLE JOHN. Right. I'm really enjoying being one of your Merry Men, Robin!

ROBIN. Good, good. Just keep your voice down.

LITTLE JOHN. Am I being too merry?

ROBIN. No. No.

LITTLE JOHN. I'm taking it too literally.

ROBIN. You're just the right amount of merry.

LITTLE JOHN. Thanks, Robin. You always know what to say.

> (**LITTLE JOHN** *moves away.* **SHIRLEY** *comes to* **MARIAN/ROBIN**'s *other side.*)

SHIRLEY. Marian.

ROBIN. Shirley. Please don't call me that. I'm in disguise.

SHIRLEY. Sorry. Robin Hood.

ROBIN. I'm actually pretending to be an old man.

SHIRLEY. Right. Right. I'll start again.

ALANNA. Now might be a good time to explain. So you know Robin Hood? The real original Robin Hood was actually Maid Marian in disguise. It's true. I was there. I am there now. But I don't know this yet. I'm just barely out of earshot. And I'm concentrating very hard on being a good archer. This is my concentrating face.

> (**ALANNA** *goes back to concentrating.*)

SHIRLEY. Old man!

ROBIN. Yes.

SHIRLEY. Old man, Prince John has been looking around for Lady Marian and he's getting suspicious. It might help if you – she were to put in an appearance. He seems very put out. And when Prince John is put out...well, I don't have to tell you.

ROBIN. Okay.

SHIRLEY. I offered to distract him, but you know how he is.

ROBIN. Yes, Shirley.

SHIRLEY. You know what I mean by distract?

ROBIN. I do.

SHIRLEY. "Surely, yes," I said. He said "Surely no." And then "Stop, Shirley." And then, "Keep your hands to yourself."

ROBIN. Very well. Very well. *(Loudly, as old man.)* I got to go see a horse about peeing somewhere. If you gentlemen...and lady will be so kind as to excuse my old withered bones for at least half of a shake. Maybe a few withered shakes thither.

> *(**MARIAN/ROBIN** transforms quickly into **LADY MARIAN** as **SHIRLEY** blocks her from view, or offstage as **ALANNA** speaks. When she is transformed, **MARIAN** goes and sits beside **PRINCE JOHN**.)*

ALANNA. I am in the zone. And I am shooting well. I will make it into the next round. Almost certainly. And then, I will be the first woman ever to win and probably Robin Hood himself will ask me if I want to be a Merry Man and then... I'm getting ahead of myself. I concentrate on my concentrating. One arrow at a time. Be in the moment, Alanna. *(She narrates as she fires an arrow.)* I pull back and "thunk." Almost. Almost. But I'm no Robin Hood. *(She sighs.)*

> *(**MARIAN** has arrived at **PRINCE JOHN**'s side.)*

PRINCE JOHN. Marian, where have you been? It's been so dreadfully boring. They just shoot at the targets, shoot at the targets over and over. No bleeding, no screaming. And they're all so common in their rags and their dirt all over, and the smells. You know how I hate that.

MARIAN. I know, my liege.

PRINCE JOHN. I've been looking at ugly things. All this ugliness. Why have you been hiding? There was nothing beautiful at all. Now I get to look at you.

MARIAN. Your highness is too kind.

PRINCE JOHN. Yes. It's one of my faults. But answer the question.

MARIAN. What question, my king?

PRINCE JOHN. Where have you been hiding yourself?

MARIAN. I had a woman issue, my liege.

PRINCE JOHN. *(Upset.)* Okay. Okay. That's enough. I didn't ask for details.

MARIAN. *(Pretending to mishear.)* Your highness wants details?

PRINCE JOHN. No details! No details!

MARIAN. Who do you favor, my liege?

PRINCE JOHN. Why you, my lady.

MARIAN. For the contest, your highness.

PRINCE JOHN. Oh right. The archery. I guess the Sheriff of Nottingham. What a boor. As long as Lady Alanna doesn't win. Whysoever did I allow a woman to shoot? Disgusting. Who do you favor?

MARIAN. Why the Sheriff, of course. If he does not win, I shall weep and weep.

PRINCE JOHN. Let's not get carried away. The feminine sex is a ridiculous sex.

MARIAN. Your highness is very wise. Why does his highness not shoot?

PRINCE JOHN. I really don't like to get my hands dirty, as you know. Filth! Anyway, it wouldn't be fair. Because I am the king chosen by God himself, I would of course win. Wherever my arrow struck, well that would be the new bullseye.

MARIAN. I did not know that.

PRINCE JOHN. Indeed. Of course if my brother – Let's not talk about him. Crusades? I said, "That's a wonderful idea." "I'll stay here and be king, but you have fun on your crusading."

MARIAN. Is he having fun?

PRINCE JOHN. Well, he's not dead yet. Once Richard is dead they will say, "The king is dead. Long live the king." And that will be me. I'll be a proper king.

MARIAN. Oh but you are already a proper king.

PRINCE JOHN. A proper king should have a queen.

> (**PRINCE JOHN** *leers. Trumpets sound, signaling the next part.*)

MARIAN. I must off.

PRINCE JOHN. Stay here and watch the rest with me. You can hold the royal hand.

MARIAN. I would like nothing better. It's just that I have to powder –

PRINCE JOHN. Don't tell me any details!!

MARIAN. – my unmentionables.

PRINCE JOHN. I asked you not to tell me! Very well. You are excused for your woman things. Blecht. Blaaach! Ugh! Eeek. *(He spits the bad taste out of his mouth.)*

> (*Near* **PRINCE JOHN, GUARD 1,** *and* **SIR LENNY THE OBSERVANT.** *They stand still, guarding, but they chat because they are bored.*)

SIR LENNY. Hey! Do you think Maid Marian looks kinda like Robin Hood?

GUARD 1. No.

> (*Back at the archery line,* **SHIRLEY** *approaches the* **SHERIFF.***)*

SHIRLEY. *(Flirty.)* Good shootin', Sheriff.

SHERIFF. I know.

SHIRLEY. I love your confidence.

SHERIFF. You love my gifts.

SHIRLEY. You have a bauble for little Shirley?

SHERIFF. Of course. But I'm of a mind not to give it to you at all.

SHIRLEY. *(Pouting.)* Why not?

SHERIFF. I see you lavishing attention on the other archers.

SHIRLEY. What? That old man? It was a pity lavish.

SHERIFF. It better be.

SHIRLEY. You're so jealous. *(She says this like it's a good thing.)* But you have no right to be. There's no ring on this finger. This Shirley is a free agent.

SHERIFF. Don't flirt with old men in front of me. Not unless you want me to jail him.

SHIRLEY. Oooh.

SHERIFF. Or hang him.

SHIRLEY. Ahhh.

SHERIFF. I'm a very powerful man.

SHIRLEY. I know. With a powerful body.

SHERIFF. Don't cross me.

SHIRLEY. I wouldn't ever. Not never. Now where's my bauble?

> *(The **SHERIFF** gives her a ring. She squeals and puts it on. She runs off admiring it.)*

SHERIFF. And stay away from that friar!

> *(The **SHERIFF** resumes shooting. The other archers have been shooting. [Optional staging if the **SHERIFF** and **FRIAR TUCK** are not played by the same actor: Behind the **SHERIFF**, we see **SHIRLEY** run into the arms of **TUCK**, recognizable because he's in a brown robe. They run off together, hand in hand.])*

> *(Meanwhile, **PRINCE JOHN** talks to one of his men, a knight called **SIR THEO THE PUNCTUAL**.)*

PRINCE JOHN. What report have you? Have you seen 'im?

SIR THEO. Who, Robin Hood?

PRINCE JOHN. Of course Robin Hood. Who else?

SIR THEO. No. No. Maybe he's not here. Just decided not to come maybe.

PRINCE JOHN. He's here. Has to show off. He's greedy. He wants all the love of all the people all the time. Love that should more properly be given to their king.

SIR THEO. Oh but the people do love you, sire.

PRINCE JOHN. Do they?

SIR THEO. Sure?

PRINCE JOHN. And Robin Hood?

SIR THEO. I'm not sure *he* loves you.

PRINCE JOHN. No. Where is he?

SIR THEO. Oh. I don't know.

PRINCE JOHN. How about a tall man? Have you seen a tall man?

SIR THEO. A big bloke? Oh yeah there's a big bloke.

PRINCE JOHN. Who was he talking to?

SIR THEO. Well I don't know where he is now, but he was talking to the old man.

PRINCE JOHN. The old man?

SIR THEO. Yes, the big bloke was talking to the old man who happens to be a particularly good archer.

(A beat.)

PRINCE JOHN. Do I need to explain it to you?

SIR THEO. Explain what?

PRINCE JOHN. Robin Hood is the old man in disguise and the very large man? That is Little John.

SIR THEO. Ohhh! I think you wanted me to look out for that very personage. So you want me to what? Arrest 'im?

PRINCE JOHN. Wait until the final shot and then, yes! Seize him.

SIR THEO. Okay but he's really big. It'll take quite a few men.

PRINCE JOHN. Not Little John. I mean yes, Little John too, but primarily, Robin Hood.

SIR THEO. Robin Hood! You think he's here?

PRINCE JOHN. Let me explain it again.

SIR THEO. Good! I'm a great listener.

(Meanwhile, the archers are shooting.)

ALANNA. The finals. I'm shooting to win. It's just me, The Sheriff of Nottingham and the old man. We're all shooting at the same target.

> (*The* **SHERIFF** *shoots. The crowd cheers.*)

It's a good shot. Can I do better? (*She aims and fires. The crowd cheers.*) Bullseye.

> (*The* **SHERIFF** *frowns.*)

I've won! Have I won? The old man still has a turn.

> (**MARIAN/ROBIN** *shoots. Looks away before the arrow hits. Whistles nonchalantly.*)

Then the old man splits my arrow with his own! My arrow falls and the old man's sticks to the middle of the bullseye. I've lost. The crowd goes crazy. No one has ever seen anything like it. The old man is surely the best archer in the country, perhaps the world, perhaps ever, perhaps always.

> (*Crowd cheers.*)

ROBIN. (*As old man.*) Where did it land? My sight isn't what it used to be.

ALANNA. Then all kinds of chaos breaks out.

PRINCE JOHN. Seize him!

ROBIN. (*As old man.*) What's happening?

> (**SIR THEO THE PUNCTUAL** *and* **SIR LENNY THE OBSERVANT** *tear away* **MARIAN/ROBIN**'s *old man disguise. Underneath, it appears to be* **ROBIN**, *in all green, with her green Robin Hood hat.*)

SHIRLEY. Robin Hood! Who woulda thought?!

ALANNA. It's not so bad to lose an archery contest to Robin Hood.

> (*They have* **ROBIN** *at swordpoint. It looks like she's doomed. The other* **GUARDS** *close in. And*

then the **MERRY MEN** *enter, big sacks of gold in tow, swinging swords. A big sword fight. On one side, the* **MERRY MEN** *like* **LITTLE JOHN, WILL SCARLETT, MUCH THE MILLER'S SON, TOMMY OF NO CONSEQUENCE,** *and* **FRIAR TUCK,** *and on the other side the* **SHERIFF, SIR THEO, SIR LENNY,** *and other* **GUARDS.** *Everybody is sword fighting.* **ROBIN** *is shooting arrows. The* **GUARDS** *enter, arrows hidden in their hands blocked from audience view. When* **ROBIN** *"shoots," they turn to the audience with the arrows held against them as if the arrows becomes visible in that second. The* **GUARDS** *fall, other* **GUARDS** *drag them offstage, and they re-enter, seemingly as different* **GUARDS,** *who* **ROBIN** *shoots. And the process is repeated. It should seem like an endless supply of* **GUARDS.***)*

ROBIN. We're outnumbered, Little John. Take the gold and run. I'll cover your escape.

LITTLE JOHN. I can't leave you.

ROBIN. Go. Take the other Merry Men. I'll find a way to escape. I always do.

LITTLE JOHN. But what if this time you can't?

ROBIN. Go. That's an order.

> **(LITTLE JOHN** *and the* **MERRY MEN** *exit. With the bags of gold. The* **GUARDS** *close in on* **ROBIN.***)*

PRINCE JOHN. Well well well. Guess you're not as clever as they say, Robin Hood.

ROBIN. I suppose not.

PRINCE JOHN. Chain him up in the high tower. Say goodbye to this outlaw. You will never see him again!! Never!! Never again! Never. Never ever. Never ever ever ever ever ever ever ever!! ...Ever!

> **(ROBIN** *is led away.* **PRINCE JOHN** *exits in another direction, triumphant.)*

ALANNA. *(Watching* **ROBIN.***)* I watched Robin go, a pain in my ribcage I couldn't quite name. I tried to make the face that went with this strange feeling but then I remembered decorum. And that I was always being watched.

2

The Prince's Chamber

*(**PRINCE JOHN** and the **SHERIFF** enter, arguing.)*

PRINCE JOHN. All of the gold? Why wasn't anyone guarding the vault?

SHERIFF. I mean there were a couple – We were concentrating on finding Robin Hood.

PRINCE JOHN. Why does this keep happening?

SHERIFF. I don't know, sire.

PRINCE JOHN. Am I not motivating you properly? Do you need threat of death over your head?

SHERIFF. No. No. I'm good.

PRINCE JOHN. *(Stifling a sob.)* I feel so empty. Exposed. Nude, even. Came in here and just took all the gold. I need that gold.

SHERIFF. I know you do.

PRINCE JOHN. YOU DON'T KNOW!

SHERIFF. I –

PRINCE JOHN. I need security. Just a little gold hidden away. For the hard times. I need it!!

SHERIFF. But surely your highness has vaults in every castle in the country.

PRINCE JOHN. That's not the point! I need it all. I need all of the money. I require it. It keeps me sane. It keeps us afloat. You don't understand. No one understands me.

SHERIFF. I understand.

PRINCE JOHN. Raise the taxes. We'll have that gold back soon.

SHERIFF. But the people. If you raise the taxes again, there could be a rebellion.

PRINCE JOHN. Nonsense. They will pay. And they will love me while they pay. I am their king. It is their duty.

SHERIFF. But –

PRINCE JOHN. Don't talk back!

SHERIFF. I wasn't gonna.

PRINCE JOHN. It looked like you were gonna talk back.

SHERIFF. No, I was just going to say, "Yes, sire." And then I was gonna agree. And then I was gonna say, "Hey you want to go jeer at Robin Hood?"

3

The Tower Prison

*(In the hall outside the prison, **GUARD 1** and **GUARD 2** stand guard.)*

GUARD 1. Okay so in this scenario, you're accused of treason, but it's a mistake. You didn't do it but no one believes you. Do you run off to Sherwood Forest to live with the Merry Men or do you hang?

GUARD 2. Can I run off somewhere else?

GUARD 1. No. It's Sherwood Forest or death. Those are the choices.

GUARD 2. Sherwood? Sure wouldn't.

*(**ALANNA** enters.)*

ALANNA. I'm just going to walk by you now.

*(The **GUARDS** wave her through.)*

GUARD 1. Lots of rubberneckers.

GUARD 2. I'd like to rubber neck her.

GUARD 1. Okay. Kill, Bed, Marry. Shirley, Marian, Alanna.

GUARD 2. Are we really not going to talk about what happened last night?

*(In the prison, **MARIAN/ROBIN**'s hands are chained to the wall, above her head. **ALANNA** enters, speaks to the audience.)*

ALANNA. Strictly speaking, I'm not supposed to be in the tower prison. I guess I just had to see him. I'm afraid my face is doing all kinds of things I don't want it to. But it goes where I go.

ROBIN. You! Hey!

ALANNA. Hello Mr. Robin Hood.

ROBIN. I know you. That was some good shooting.

ALANNA. Oh! Really? Thank you! Really?

ROBIN. You have the potential to be great.

ALANNA. You think so?

ROBIN. Yes. Say, could you do me a favor? My hat, it's –

ALANNA. You want me to move your hat?

ROBIN. Could you? Maybe just take it off? I thought I'd be able to reach it but I can't quite reach it.

ALANNA. *(Rushes over.)* Sure. Of course.

> *(***ALANNA*** *removes* ***MARIAN/ROBIN****'s hat. A magical sound. A harp? Her hair comes undone.)*

Lady Marian, is that you?

MARIAN. That's not really important. Could you maybe just put that hairpin in my hand?

ALANNA. The what?

MARIAN. Hairpin! Hairpin!

> *(***ALANNA*** *hands her the hairpin.* ***MARIAN*** *picks the locks of her shackles with the hairpin and then her hands are free. She removes her other Robin clothing and she is full* ***MARIAN*** *again. She holds the Robin clothes in her hands. She starts to leave.)*

Thanks! I owe you one.

ALANNA. Wait! Where are you going?

MARIAN. I got some business to finish in Sherwood Forest. Before they try to rescue me. Hey let's keep the whole Marian is Robin Hood thing between the two of us, okay? Great! Thanks!

ALANNA. No!

MARIAN. No?

ALANNA. I mean, take me with you.

MARIAN. To Sherwood? See the thing is –

ALANNA. I want to be one of the Merry Men.

MARIAN. But you're a woman.

ALANNA. So are you.

MARIAN. Well… You'd have to pretend to be a man.

ALANNA. Why's that?

MARIAN. That's how it works.

ALANNA. So I can join then?

MARIAN. Well –

> (*Enter* **PRINCE JOHN** *and the* **SHERIFF.**)

PRINCE JOHN. Marian, here you are. Wait, where's Robin Hood?! I said the tower prison.

SHERIFF. But I did put him in the tower...uh-oh.

PRINCE JOHN. Guards!

> (**GUARD 1** *and* **GUARD 2** *rush in.*)

Did you do this, Marian?!

MARIAN. Me? How? Why?

PRINCE JOHN. I hear you're very close.

ALANNA. You have no idea.

MARIAN. He was leaping from the tower window as I came in.

PRINCE JOHN. Are those his clothes?

MARIAN. He was nude.

> (*They all go to the "window" and look down. Except* **GUARD 1.**)

ALANNA. It's true. I saw it too.

GUARD 1. Nude? Is it true what they say about his, uh, you know?

ALANNA. Oh. Yes. Robin Hood. Yes, very much.

> (**GUARD 1** *runs to the window too.*)

PRINCE JOHN. He can't have survived. Dredge the moat! Search the grounds! Marian, we'll discuss this later.

> (*The* **GUARDS** *run off.* **PRINCE JOHN** *and the* **SHERIFF** *exit, agitated.*)

4

Sherwood Forest

(Along a road, **MARIAN** *and* **ALANNA** *are changing into men's clothes.* **MARIAN/ROBIN** *already wears the Robin Hood hat.* **TANNER** *enters, sees them.)*

TANNER. Robin! What are you doing?

ROBIN. We were in disguise.

TANNER. You with all your plots and plans. But I guess they work don't they? Little John just gave me a sack of gold coins. Bless your work. Bless you a thousand times. It's so hard to get ahead no matter how hard I work. Gotta keep out of the poor house. Or worse.

ALANNA. What's worse?

TANNER. That is the question, isn't it? *(To* **ROBIN.***)* How's Marian? You lock that down yet?

ROBIN. Not yet.

TANNER. Marry that girl. A girl like that gots lotsa options. Believe me.

ROBIN. I believe you.

TANNER. Not like us. Lotsa options. And so pretty. Not like us. Why even the Prince has been taking notice. And you know what they say – when the Prince takes notice...

ALANNA. What?

TANNER. You better lock it down.

ROBIN. Indeed. I thank you. I will heed your advice.

TANNER. Be sure you do.

ROBIN. Now we must off to the Merry Men. We are missed.

TANNER. Such nice boys. Be careful. There's outlaws in this forest. *(Laughs.)* Outlaws! Ha!

5

Farther Into Sherwood Forest

(The **MERRY MEN** *are singing.* **LITTLE JOHN, WILL SCARLETT, MUCH THE MILLER'S SON, FRIAR TUCK, TOMMY OF NO CONSEQUENCE.***)*

MERRY MEN.
WE ARE THE MERRY MEN
WE STEAL AGAIN AND AGAIN
AND AGAIN AND AGAIN
AND AGAIN AND AGAIN
WE ARE THE MERRY MEN

WE ARE THE MERRY MEN
WE LAUGH AND LAUGH AND THEN
AGAIN AND AGAIN
AND AGAIN AND AGAIN
WE ARE THE MERRY MEN
AGAIN!

(They sing until **ROBIN** *and* **ALANNA** *arrive.* **ALANNA** *is now dressed like a man.* **ROBIN** *is back in all Robin clothes.)*

ROBIN. Merry Men! How I've missed you during my long incarceration! It's been hours.

MERRY MEN. *(Ad lib.)* Robin! Yay!

LITTLE JOHN. Who's this, Robin?

ROBIN. This is Alan à Dale. *[Pronounced Alan "uh" Dale.]*

ALANNA. *(As man.)* Pleasure. Pleasure.

*(***ALANNA** *starts to curtsy, then remembers and bows.)*

ROBIN. He helped me escape. He wants to be one of us.

WILL. Does he now?

ROBIN. This is –

WILL. Scarlett. I mean, Will Scarlett. My name is Will.

ALANNA. Hi.

WILL. Hi.

ALANNA. Hi.

WILL. Hi.

> *(There's something going on there. Some kind of instant chemistry. That makes them both nervous. Probably a musical "fall in love" moment during the "Hi's.")*

ALANNA. And suddenly, I can't feel my face.

ROBIN. And this is Much the Miller's son.

> *(**ALANNA** snaps out of it.)*

MUCH. Any friend of Robin's –

ROBIN. Friar Tuck.

TUCK. Can I get you a tankard of ale?

ALANNA. Thank you.

ROBIN. He likes his drink.

TOMMY. And I'm Tommy of No Consequence. It's okay if you haven't heard of me.

ROBIN. So what do you say? Can he be one of us?

LITTLE JOHN. Let's see what he's made of.

WILL. Yes, let's do that.

> *(**WILL** and **ALANNA** stare at each other.)*

How are you with a sword?

> *(**WILL** tosses a sword. **ALANNA** catches it. They sword fight. It's intense. **ALANNA** disarms **WILL**, has **WILL** at swordpoint on the ground. They look at each other for a few seconds. **WILL** pushes the blade away. Gets up.)*

(Grabbing two staffs.) Okay but how are you with a quarterstaff?

ALANNA. I do okay.

LITTLE JOHN. Usually we take turns. You want me to –

ROBIN. Just let it happen.

(**WILL** *and* **ALANNA** *fight with quarterstaffs. Quarterstaves? They fight with long sticks. Just as intense. Finally,* **ALANNA** *knocks* **WILL** *down.*)

ALANNA. You want to see me with a bow? I'm a good shot.

ROBIN. I think you've proven yourself. Break up into patrols. The Sheriff's men are bound to be in Sherwood soon, looking for me. Why don't you ambush them and make them feel foolish...like we do? Alan, Will, why don't you two work together. I think we've got a good team there.

(**WILL** *and* **ALANNA** *look at each other. Everyone looks at them.* **SHIRLEY** *enters, out of breath.*)

SHIRLEY. Robin! Smithy's gone missing!

ROBIN. The blacksmith?

SHIRLEY. The same. He's been disappeared.

(*The mood darkens.*)

ROBIN. Take some gold to distribute to the poor. John and I will plot and plan about these disappearances. Go!

(*All but* **ROBIN** *and* **LITTLE JOHN** *exit.*)

6

(In another part of the forest, **MUCH** *and* **TOMMY** *patrol.)*

TOMMY. I've been thinking, Much.

MUCH. Please don't do that, Tommy.

TOMMY. If I did something important. Maybe I'll be remembered in the stories and the songs. And they can call me Tommy of Some Consequence.

MUCH. Tommy, don't get yourself killed. I mean not for nothing.

TOMMY. No, but what if I do something heroic?

MUCH. You worry me when you talk.

TOMMY. I know.

MUCH. Tommy, do you ever feel like you don't quite fit in?

TOMMY. All the time, Much. All the time. I'm not like you.

MUCH. *(Angst.)* Right. Yeah. Yeah. I didn't mean me. I was just...nevermind. Nevermind.

7

(Back with **ROBIN** *and* **LITTLE JOHN.***)*

LITTLE JOHN. What are we gonna do Robin? About the disappearances?

ROBIN. I think we need to think about it.

LITTLE JOHN. Thinking's not my strong suit.

ROBIN. I know, Little John. But you have lots of other strong suits.

LITTLE JOHN. Most of my suits are strong.

ROBIN. Indeed.

LITTLE JOHN. You know I always think best when I'm wrestling.

ROBIN. I know, Little John.

(They square off and begin to wrestle.)

LITTLE JOHN. I also sometimes say things I don't mean to say when we wrestle.

ROBIN. I know, Little John.

LITTLE JOHN. It makes me feel big.

*(***LITTLE JOHN*** may pick up* **ROBIN** *over his head.)*

You're getting better.

ROBIN. Thank you.

8

(In another, other part of the forest. **WILL** *and* **ALANNA** *patrol.)*

WILL. We may as well get to know each other. We'll be out here a while. You want to tell me about yourself?

ALANNA. I suppose.

WILL. Or not.

ALANNA. *(Disappointed.)* Oh.

WILL. Fine. Tell me about yourself. No. I don't care. Are you gonna tell me about yourself?

ALANNA. I want to tell you enough for you to like me but not enough to embarrass myself. There are ways probably to do that. To hide behind a disguise.

WILL. What you need to know about me isn't just my skill with weaponry or that I move silent like a cat. I'm not the merriest man but I never thought that's what it was about.

ALANNA. What are you then?

WILL. I am the most mysterious.

ALANNA. No.

WILL. The deadliest.

ALANNA. Nah.

WILL. I am the most Will Scarlett.

ALANNA. You sure are. *(To audience.)* I think if I pay very close attention, I can tell anything just by looking closely enough at someone's face. My eyes are like knives.

*(**ALANNA** stares at **WILL**. **WILL** stares back.)*

WILL. You're staring.

ALANNA. Yes.

9

(**MUCH** *and* **TOMMY** *are apart, with bows drawn, facing opposite directions.*)

MUCH. Do you hear something?

TOMMY. Maybe.

(*Two* **GUARDS** *come. They throw a black bag over* **TOMMY***'s head and carry him away.* **MUCH** *doesn't see this.*)

MUCH. Tommy?! Tommy!

(**ANOTHER GUARD** *or the* **SAME GUARD** *arrives from another direction with another black bag in hand.* **MUCH** *turns and shoots him with an arrow. The* **GUARD** *falls, dead. He may or may not scream before dying.*)

10

(Back to **ROBIN** *and* **LITTLE JOHN**. *They wrestle.)*

LITTLE JOHN. Sometimes when we wrestle, I think about Maid Marian.

ROBIN. I know, Little John.

LITTLE JOHN. Tell me about her.

ROBIN. She's a person, like anyone else.

LITTLE JOHN. But she's soft. So soft.

ROBIN. Not softer than me.

LITTLE JOHN. Much softer. What is it like when she kisses you?

ROBIN. I don't know.

LITTLE JOHN. Is it like snowfall? Is it like leaves? Is it like falling in a river or hitting your head on a tree?

ROBIN. Yes.

LITTLE JOHN. I knew it. She's really special. Especially special. You're lucky to have her.

ROBIN. *(Sadly.)* I know, Little John.

LITTLE JOHN. I'm going to stop thinking about her now. Right now. Now. Now. Now. Now. Okay, really. Now. Say something nice the next time you see her. Like...I send my regards. So she knows I care in a respectful way.

ROBIN. Okay, Little John.

LITTLE JOHN. I guess we should think more about the problem at hand.

(Pause.)

Do you think the disappeared are dead now?

ROBIN. I think he's collecting them. I think he's taunting me.

LITTLE JOHN. What will we do?

ROBIN. Well we'll break them out of jail, won't we? It's time to plan a jailbreak.

LITTLE JOHN. Oh good!

11

(Back to **ALANNA** *and* **WILL**. *They stare at each other until* **WILL** *breaks the gaze and moves away.)*

ALANNA. You're very graceful.

WILL. What?

ALANNA. I didn't think you'd move so gracefully.

WILL. Are you calling me unmanly?

ALANNA. What if I was?

WILL. Then I'd kick in your teeth.

ALANNA. I'd like to see you try.

WILL. I went easy on you back there because of your youth. I won't make that mistake again.

ALANNA. Ha!

WILL. What's that?

ALANNA. That's me laughing at you. Ha! I just did it again.

*(***WILL*** launches herself at* **ALANNA**. *They tumble. It's violent. Maybe a punch or two land. Then they are kissing.)*

We should stop.

WILL. It's fine.

ALANNA. I don't think it is.

WILL. It is. I'll tell you why later.

(This is good enough for **ALANNA**. *They continue kissing.)*

12

*(**TUCK** and **SHIRLEY** in Shirley's bed.)*

TUCK. I want you all to myself all the time.

SHIRLEY. Can't do it. Anyway, don't you have to do God things?

TUCK. Let's not worry about that too much. I have time for you.

SHIRLEY. Don't be greedy.

TUCK. It's not greed. But even if it is. I'm okay with it. I'll take on whatever sins I have to.

SHIRLEY. That's not very holy.

TUCK. I do holy my way. I help the poor by stealing. And by beating in the heads of the Sheriff's men. And I enjoy what God has to offer. A sunny day. A barrel of ale. You.

SHIRLEY. What I need is to be taken care of. Worshipped even. It's not what I want. It's just the position I'm in. The positions I like to be in. You're a good man and I like to spend time with you because of your goodness. But that doesn't mean you give me enough. It'll take more than you for me to get everything I need.

TUCK. Maybe things will be different tomorrow.

SHIRLEY. Maybe. No. Maybe.

TUCK. Want to go one more time?

SHIRLEY. Yes, Friar.

TUCK. Say it again.

SHIRLEY. Yes, Friar.

(They dive under the covers.)

13

Outside The Prince's Bedchamber

*(**GUARD 1** and **GUARD 2** stand guarding.)*

GUARD 1. Which one?

GUARD 2. Lucy.

GUARD 1. His favorite. I think brief and rhythmic. Loud finish.

GUARD 2. I say longer than normal and then he faints and accidentally says his brother's name.

GUARD 1. The usual wager?

GUARD 2. The usual wager.

14

The Prince's Bedchamber

(**PRINCE JOHN** *in bed with* **LUCY**, *a concubine.*
PRINCE JOHN *is finishing.*)

PRINCE JOHN. UHHHNGng!

(*He rolls off.*)

I did it again! Perfectly.

LUCY. Thank you, your majesty.

PRINCE JOHN. 'Twas nothing.

LUCY. Your majesty is too kind to me.

PRINCE JOHN. Yes. Most likely. Okay, now clean up and go.

LUCY. Your majesty, I have a question I wish to ask.

PRINCE JOHN. (*Sighs.*) All right. Fine.

LUCY. My mother wishes to know...or rather, I wonder if
it's okay to say...may I tell people that I'm your favorite
concubine, sire?

PRINCE JOHN. Why is everyone so greedy?! Isn't it enough to
be one of the concubines? Must you create hierarchies?

LUCY. No, sire. I apologize, sire.

PRINCE JOHN. Isn't it enough we share our royal bed with
you? I let you bathe and live at the castle whenever I'm
in town.

LUCY. Yes, your majesty.

PRINCE JOHN. You get a regular audience with the king.

LUCY. Which reminds me, will you please tell me where my
father has been taken?

PRINCE JOHN. No, I will not. Be happy with your lot in life.
You are favored by the king.

LUCY. The favorite?

PRINCE JOHN. Do you want to follow your father wherever
he went?

LUCY. No sire.

PRINCE JOHN. We will not speak on this again.

LUCY. Yes, sire.

PRINCE JOHN. I was too harsh to you just now, wasn't I? Take a jewel from the jewel spittoon on your way out.

LUCY. Am I to leave, your highness?

PRINCE JOHN. Exit! Exit!

> (**LUCY** *exits, taking a jewel on her way out. There is a knock.*)

Enter!

> (**SIR THEO** *enters, leading* **TOMMY**, *who still has a bag over his head.* **SIR LENNY** *follows.*)

SIR THEO. We managed to capture a Merry Man, sire.

> (**SIR THEO** *removes the bag.*)

TOMMY. This is a nice room.

PRINCE JOHN. This one's of no consequence.

TOMMY. I know.

SIR LENNY. He could be of some consequence maybe.

PRINCE JOHN. We could hang him but will Robin Hood even show up for the hanging?

TOMMY. He might show up.

PRINCE JOHN. And if he does, will you actually be able to capture him?

SIR THEO. We're working on doing better.

PRINCE JOHN. You need to do better at doing better.

SIR THEO & SIR LENNY. Yes, sire.

PRINCE JOHN. I need a new plan. The higher taxes won't stop him from robbing me again. And again. And you're useless.

TOMMY. Maybe I can help.

PRINCE JOHN. Did he just say something?

TOMMY. I want to be of some consequence.

PRINCE JOHN. *(Gives him a once-over, and then.)* I don't see it.

TOMMY. I could be a spy maybe. I could say I escaped and then find out the new plans and then send you messages with carrier pigeons or tied to arrows shot over your wall. If you just give me a chance – I think I could be a double agent to the crown. You could call me. Double Oh Tommy. The Double Agent Of Some Consequence.

PRINCE JOHN. *(Thinks.)* Hmmm. Hmmm. Hmmm. Hmm. No. That's all ridiculous. Laughable. I don't need the help of someone so low. Take him away.

TOMMY. But I can be someone.

PRINCE JOHN. No.

> *(**SIR THEO** drags **TOMMY** off.)*

Where is Marian? Find me Marian. She's always not around.

SIR LENNY. I noticed that.

PRINCE JOHN. Who is allowing her to roam freely all over the kingdom?

SIR LENNY. Ladies be ladies.

PRINCE JOHN. Do they still say she spends time with Robin Hood?

SIR LENNY. I have heard murmurs. But no one ever sees them together.

PRINCE JOHN. If I hanged her he would show up.

SIR LENNY. Indeed.

PRINCE JOHN. But maybe there is another way to skin the cat.

SIR LENNY. There are fifteen ways that I know of. Using knives I mean.

PRINCE JOHN. You should leave now before I make you stab yourself.

> *(Exit **SIR LENNY**.)*

15

Sherwood Forest

> (**ALANNA** *and* **WILL**, *kissing. They stop. Look at each other.*)

ALANNA. *(To audience.)* I look into his eyes and I see deception so when he says –

WILL. I don't want you to think you're special or anything. I do this all the time.

ALANNA. *(To audience.)* I don't believe him. But I feel the tiny daggers he has thrown and they hurt all the same.

WILL. I just don't want you to get too attached. Merry Men come and Merry Men go. You're no different.

ALANNA. *(To audience.)* "I'm sorry you've been hurt," I say. Because that's what I see.

WILL. Not me. Never me. I'm the heartbreaker.

ALANNA. *(To audience.)* But before anything more ludicrous can come out of his mouth, I speak. It goes from my body directly to my mouth without passing through my brain. I say –

(To **WILL**.*)* I have just now fallen completely and utterly in love with you and to make matters worse, I am telling you.

> (**WILL** *turns away.*)

(To audience.) He says nothing. And a silence descends. And in the silence, I feel the danger into which my mouth has led me once again. Perhaps this is finally the end of me. It feels that way. I sit a minute with that feeling of nothingness. I could learn to not exist if I had to, I think. And then he turns and says –

WILL. Come on. We have some patrolling to do.

ALANNA. *(To audience.)* But instead he kisses me again.

> *(They kiss.)*

And the kiss says, "I love you, desperately, wholly,

individually, always." But that's not what he says. He says –

    (They kiss.)

WILL. Okay. We'll do it your way.

16

The Sheriff's Chamber In Nottingham Castle

(The **SHERIFF** *and* **SHIRLEY** *in bed.)*

SHIRLEY. What I need is to be taken care of. Worshipped even. It's not what I want. It's just the position I'm in. The positions I like to be in. You're a powerful man and I like to spend time with you because of your power. But that doesn't mean you give me enough. It'll take more than you for me to get everything I need.

SHERIFF. I can be enough.

SHIRLEY. I dunno.

SHERIFF. It's Robin Hood, isn't it? When we catch him and hang him, then you'll see how powerful I can be.

SHIRLEY. Robin Hood is uncatchable.

SHERIFF. You'll see. When I catch him, you will see.

SHIRLEY. Let's go to the dungeons.

SHERIFF. Why you want to do that?

SHIRLEY. *(Sexy.)* Are they dirty and musty with rats and chains and rusty torture devices?

SHERIFF. Yes but they are full of prisoners.

SHIRLEY. They can watch. We'll give 'em a thrill. You have a map of the underground dungeons?

SHERIFF. What for?

SHIRLEY. I like to plan my escapades. Where's the rack?

SHERIFF. *(Opens scroll.)* All right. Well. This part is full of poachers. None of them have hands.

SHIRLEY. Oooh.

SHERIFF. And the scum in this part owe taxes. It's costing an arm and a leg to keep them alive. They're really just bait for Robin Hood though.

SHIRLEY. Bait for Robin Hood?

SHERIFF. It's ingenious, actually. If you try to enter the room without pulling the lever, rows and rows of crossbows appear and shoot at the entrance.

SHIRLEY. Oooh.

SHERIFF. You're not interested in this.

SHIRLEY. Oh, but I am. *(Kisses his neck.)* Is there another way into the room?

17

Another Part Of Sherwood

(**ALANNA** *and* **WILL** *entangled.*)

ALANNA. I feel like we're not doing a good job of patrolling.

WILL. This is a perfect vantage point. I can hear and see them coming from miles away.

ALANNA. But you're looking at me.

WILL. I look away, now and again.

ALANNA. Do you?

WILL. When you blink.

ALANNA. There's something I should say.

WILL. To me? You better not say it. I don't do well with moments like that.

ALANNA. I don't want there to be secrets between us.

WILL. I'm okay with secrets between us.

ALANNA. I need you to know. I'm not a man.

WILL. Oh.

ALANNA. I'm a woman.

WILL. You are? I'm a woman too.

ALANNA. Oh. So we're not... I thought. I was a woman and you were a man.

WILL. I thought I was the woman.

ALANNA. Huh.

WILL. Well.

ALANNA. So do you...like women.

WILL. I like women.

ALANNA. As much as men?

WILL. If that woman is you.

ALANNA. I think that's how I feel too.

(*They kiss.*)

Yes. That's how I feel too.

WILL. It's different, now that we're both women.

ALANNA. Yes. Different better or different worse?

WILL. Better.

ALANNA. I think so too.

WILL. Hold on. Let me shoot arrows at the king's men.

> (**ALANNA** *and* **WILL** *both stand and shoot arrows.*)

ALANNA. Did we get them all, Will?

WILL. I think so. You can call me Scarlett. If you want.

ALANNA. Scarlett.

> (*They drop their bows and resume kissing.*)

18

Nottingham Castle

*(**GUARD 1** and **GUARD 2** on lookout.)*

GUARD 1. I hate lookout.

GUARD 2. Look out!

GUARD 1. *(Looking around, terrified.)* What?! What?!

GUARD 2. Nothing. I just always wanted to do that.

GUARD 1. I think continuing to associate with you is bad for my career.

GUARD 2. "Look out!" *(Laughs.)*

19

Sherwood Forest

(All the **MERRY MEN. MUCH** *is telling the story of* **TOMMY**'s *disappearance.)*

MUCH. And then FOOM! He was gone.

LITTLE JOHN. Froom?

MUCH. No, more like – Foom!

LITTLE JOHN. Fume.

MUCH. Foom! Foom!

ROBIN. *(Drawing on the ground.)* They've taken Tommy of No Consequence! This will not stand. It is time to plan our prison break. Shirley is getting more detailed plans but for now, we'll approach from the north. Friar Tuck is in charge of southern diversion but the bulk of the Merry Men will approach from this point.

MUCH. Um. I'm sorry.

ROBIN. What is it, Much?

MUCH. It's the term Merry Men.

ROBIN. You're thinking why are we "Merry" when we're attacking? But we can be. I want us all to thoroughly enjoy our mischief as well as our bloodletting. Have fun out there, men.

MUCH. Actually, it's the "Men" part.

ROBIN. What do you mean?

MUCH. I'm not – I mean I don't feel like a man.

ROBIN. Okay.

MUCH. I don't want to dress like a man or talk like a man or drink like a man. Or kill like a man. I just don't identify with all that comes with manhood and manliness. So I want you all to know, I'm not a man anymore.

WILL. Are ye sayin' you're a lady, Much?

MUCH. Not a woman neither. I think that I'm not a man or a woman. Neither of those things feels like who I am.

LITTLE JOHN. What's happening, Robin?

ROBIN. So what would you like to be called?

MUCH. Just Much. I'm a person. A human being.

WILL. You're Much the Miller's Son. You can't change who you are. That's who you've always been.

MUCH. Right. That too. Don't call me Much the Miller's Son. Call me Much the Miller's Child.

ROBIN. Okay.

MUCH. And instead of saying "him" when you're talking about me, say, "they" or "them."

WILL. Are there two of you, Much?

MUCH. I know it's not ideal.

ALANNA. We could say "he/she."

MUCH. No but I'm not a "he" or a "she." Just say "they." It's fine. It'll be fine.

ROBIN. What about Merry Men then? Should I say, Merry Men and also Much?

MUCH. Maybe Merry Personages?

ALANNA. Merry People?

WILL. Wait a minute. Wait a minute. People can't just stop being one thing and start being another thing.

MUCH. That's not –

ALANNA. Yes they can. You can wake up in love. You can wake up to thinking a new way you never thought. All sorts of things could happen.

LITTLE JOHN. Can it?

ALANNA. *(To* **WILL.***)* Can I talk to you for a minute?

> (**ALANNA** *and* **WILL** *step out of earshot of the others.)*

LITTLE JOHN. Can I become a bear, then?

ROBIN. No, Little John.

ALANNA. Much's bravery has inspired me.

WILL. In what way?

ALANNA. I want to tell them. About us.

WILL. They won't understand.

ALANNA. They're our family. They'll understand.

WILL. You want to tell them you're a woman?

ALANNA. Oh no! I guess not. I really like being a man. I can do so many things as a man.

WILL. Well, I don't want to stop being a man.

ALANNA. Then we'll keep being men.

WILL. So what are we telling them?

ALANNA. That we're in love.

WILL. Oh. We're men in love?

ALANNA. You don't want to.

WILL. Well. Um. Well. Er. Well. Hmmm. Well. No. Maybe. Well. I don't know. I guess. I guess. Okay.

ALANNA. Okay?

WILL. Okay.

ALANNA. *(To audience.)* This is my brave face.

(They step back over to the others.)

Will and I have an announcement.

LITTLE JOHN. Oh no!

ALANNA. We are in love. With each other. Will and I are in romantic entanglements in serious ways.

*(**ALANNA** nudges **WILL**.)*

WILL. Yeah. It's true.

LITTLE JOHN. With each other?

ROBIN. Congratulations.

ALANNA. We just thought people should know.

ROBIN. Thank you for telling us. That's wonderful. I think everyone should be in love if they can. When there's the possibility for it. If you're fortunate. Some people are fortunate. So congrats. We are, so happy for you. And for you too Much. *(A moment.)* If there aren't any more announcements, I do think we should finish planning the prison break.

WILL. Right. Sorry.

ALANNA. Sorry.

ROBIN. There's no reason to apologize. You know what? Let's break for dinner. We'll drink to your love, and to Much for his er...their personhood.

> *(The* **MERRY MEN** *scatter.* **ALANNA** *and* **WILL** *leave, holding hands.* **LITTLE JOHN** *remains.)*

LITTLE JOHN. Robin? I don't understand what's happening.

ROBIN. Is it too much change too fast, old friend?

LITTLE JOHN. I guess so.

ROBIN. But things happen when things happen.

LITTLE JOHN. I guess you have Maid Marian and they have each other.

ROBIN. Right.

LITTLE JOHN. Sometimes it seems everybody's got someone but me.

ROBIN. No. No.

LITTLE JOHN. I don't understand these new things.

ROBIN. Right. You know, Little John, I wanted to tell you something, actually. I – you and me, I mean. No. You. You're –

LITTLE JOHN. At least I can always count on you, Robin. To stay constant.

ROBIN. You're a great asset to the team.

LITTLE JOHN. Thanks Robin. I just wish. No, nevermind. I'm looking forward to the jailbreak.

> *(***LITTLE JOHN** *exits.* **SHIRLEY** *enters, having seen the end of that. She hands* **ROBIN** *the scroll of the dungeon map.)*

SHIRLEY. Oh, Marian. You won't die in a hail of arrows. In the end, it will be loneliness that does you in.

ROBIN. *(Letting herself be a bit* **MARIAN.***)* I know.

SHIRLEY. Just tell him.

ROBIN. Little John has a lot of good traits. He's a good man, strong, handsome, honest. Handsome. Kind. Sweet.

Poetic in his way. Gentle. Loving. But Little John is not a smart man. I can't tell him because he's not smart enough to be deceitful. Prince John would have Marian swinging from the gallows in a fortnight.

SHIRLEY. I know. I just wish there was a way. To have it all.

ROBIN. Some of us have to have less so all of us can have more.

SHIRLEY. I know. I know. I just wish...

>   *(They sigh.* **ROBIN** *opens the scroll.)*

ROBIN. Me too. But right now – Marian's going to go scout this out, see if I can't mess with Prince John. Robin will set the plan in motion when I return. We attack at midnight.

SHIRLEY. I'll follow after a dalliance or two. In case you need backup. Hehe.

>   *(***ROBIN*** *nods, exits.* **FRIAR TUCK** *appears.)*

TUCK. How's the Sheriff?

SHIRLEY. Fine. How's God?

TUCK. Fine.

SHIRLEY. I hate that you have an effect on me.

TUCK. You've been thinking about me.

SHIRLEY. Maybe.

TUCK. About settling down?

SHIRLEY. I'm not the kind to settle down, but if I were...

TUCK. What?

SHIRLEY. It would be with someone like you.

TUCK. You mean with me?

SHIRLEY. Okay, yeah.

TUCK. I'll take it. My straw mattress is cold. Warm it up for me?

SHIRLEY. With pleasure.

TUCK. That's what I had in mind.

SHIRLEY. Quickly, Friar.

TUCK. Say it again.

SHIRLEY. Quickly, Friar.

      (**TUCK** *and* **SHIRLEY** *exit together.*)

20

Nottingham Castle

(**GUARD 1** *and* **GUARD 2** *are on lookout.*)

GUARD 1. I'm not sure I want to be a knight anymore.

GUARD 2. No?

GUARD 1. Working here doesn't gel with my values anymore.

GUARD 2. What would you do instead?

GUARD 1. Maybe open up a mill on a river somewhere. Ground grain.

GUARD 2. But then you wouldn't get to kill anyone anymore.

GUARD 1. There's the rub. So I stay to kill, but for how long? I have to follow my heart, take care of me too.

GUARD 2. You want too much.

GUARD 1. Maybe. Tommy of No Consequence is dead.

GUARD 2. Who's that?

GUARD 1. It doesn't matter.

GUARD 2. How'd he die?

GUARD 1. In jail.

GUARD 2. Oh. A mill, huh?

GUARD 1. Yeah. You know. I'd ground wheat. And corn.

GUARD 2. Corn!

21

The Prince's Chamber

(**PRINCE JOHN** *is fiddling with a gold coin.*
MARIAN *enters.*)

PRINCE JOHN. Marian, where have you been?

MARIAN. I took a stroll. Then while I was strolling, I took a walk. Then I wandered around.

PRINCE JOHN. Near Sherwood?

MARIAN. Heavens no. Why would I go there? There are outlaws in that forest.

PRINCE JOHN. You can't fool me, Marian. I know your secret. I know the truth about you and Robin Hood.

MARIAN. I know of no connection between me and the outlaw Hood. Have you ever seen us together?

PRINCE JOHN. Don't play games with me.

MARIAN. I ask you sincerely, highness. Do you think that he and I have...relations?

PRINCE JOHN. Relations? Ugh. However you say it. You are quite close. Too close. It is dangerous. The important thing is, it ends today.

MARIAN. Why today, sire?

PRINCE JOHN. Because today, you are engaged.

MARIAN. Am I? I must have forgotten. To whom am I engaged, sire?

PRINCE JOHN. Why, to me.

MARIAN. It is an honor I never imagined.

PRINCE JOHN. Yes, yes.

MARIAN. I am speechless. Then I am to be, the queen?

PRINCE JOHN. A princess.

MARIAN. What shall my first order of business be?

PRINCE JOHN. You're taking this well.

MARIAN. I will rule this country with an iron fist.

PRINCE JOHN. I'll take care of the ruling.

MARIAN. Highness, now that you have me, all the responsibility need not rest on your shoulders.

PRINCE JOHN. It is a lot of responsibility.

MARIAN. It makes you so tense.

PRINCE JOHN. It's that Robin Hood.

MARIAN. I know.

PRINCE JOHN. He wants all my gold and he wants you too.

MARIAN. Are you equating me with gold, sire?

PRINCE JOHN. No? Yes? You are shinier of course.

MARIAN. Does your highness insult me?

PRINCE JOHN. No. You insult me with your impertinence. Robin Hood must die. I will have his head. And I shall serve it to you on our wedding day.

MARIAN. You are too kind. Let us waste no time. Guards!

(**GUARD 1** *and* **GUARD 2** *enter.*)

Attack Sherwood Forest with all available force! Take Robin Hood by storm. Don't return until you have him! And send in Lucy to take care of his highness' tension.

(**GUARD 1** *and* **GUARD 2** *begin to exit.*)

PRINCE JOHN. Ahem. I give the orders around here. Attack Sherwood Forest with all available force! Take Robin Hood by storm. Don't return until you have him! Leave the minimum guards at the castle gates. But first, lock Lady Marian in the highest tower. You'll do no more wandering. I'm locking this down.

(**GUARD 1** *and* **GUARD 2** *seize* **MARIAN. SHIRLEY** *enters to see this.*)

GUARD 1. Yes, sire.

PRINCE JOHN. Oh and send in Lucy too.

GUARD 2. Yes sire.

(*As the* **GUARDS** *exit with* **MARIAN.**)

GUARD 1. The usual wager?

GUARD 2. Indeed.

22

Sherwood Forest

(All the **MERRY MEN** *are there, waiting.)*

LITTLE JOHN. Robin should be back by now. Should we postpone?

WILL. I hate postponing.

MUCH. We can't attack without Robin.

LITTLE JOHN. What if they got him?

ALANNA. *(To audience.)* Robin Hood could never be captured.

*(***SHIRLEY*** enters, out of breath.)*

SHIRLEY. They've captured Robin Hood!!

LITTLE JOHN. Oh no!

TUCK. We are undone.

MUCH. What are we gonna do now? Should we disband?

WILL. We're not disbanding.

MUCH. How are we going to do it without him?

ALANNA. We'll just have to rescue him as well.

SHIRLEY. Also the Sheriff's men and the King's guards are on their way to Sherwood to kill us all.

(Fear and confusion.)

ALANNA. *(Taking command.)* We leave now. Gather your wits about you and your weapons too. We will conquer with our brains and we will demolish with our mighty swords. And we will do it all for Robin Hood!

MERRY MEN & MUCH. For Robin Hood!

ALANNA. *(Unrolling the map.)* We'll backtrack around the invading forces and approach the castle from here. Tuck, here. Much, here. The rest with me! Onward! To the castle!

MERRY MEN & MUCH. To the castle!

(They exit, running.)

23

The Tower Prison

*(On the other side of the stage, **GUARD 1** and maybe **GUARD 2** are disarming **MARIAN**.)*

*(**MARIAN** gives **GUARD 1** a sword.)*

GUARD 1. And that too.

*(**MARIAN** removes a dagger from beneath her skirts and hands it to **GUARD 1**.)*

And that.

*(**MARIAN** gives him another dagger.)*

And that.

*(**MARIAN** gives him a crossbow.)*

And that.

*(**MARIAN** gives him throwing stars. A mace? Nunchucks? Afterwards, **MARIAN** moves away.)*

And the hairpins too.

*(**MARIAN** sighs and gives him the hairpins. **GUARD 1** shackles her arms in front of her. The **GUARDS** exit, locking her in. The noise of a metal door slamming shut.)*

24

The Prince's Chamber

(PRINCE JOHN and LUCY having sex.)

PRINCE JOHN. Unh. Uhn! Uhn! UHNNNN! Richard!!

LUCY. Is that it?

> *(PRINCE JOHN weeps. LUCY holds him, uncertainly.)*

25

Nottingham Castle

(**SIR LENNY** *and* **SIR THEO** *guarding the ramparts.*)

SIR LENNY. Sometimes when I see the Merry Men I get tingly. That ever happen to you?

SIR THEO. No. You mean like you're tingling to kill them?

SIR LENNY. *(No.)* Yes. Exactly. Let's speak no more of it. Hey does it look like Sherwood is moving to you?

SIR THEO. No.

SIR LENNY. Okay.

SIR THEO. Don't be stupid.

SIR LENNY. It just looks like it's moving.

SIR THEO. It's not moving.

SIR LENNY. I say it's moving and as you know I am known as Sir Lenny the Observant.

SIR THEO. It's time I told you the truth. That's an ironic moniker.

SIR LENNY. What?!

SIR THEO. I'm sorry. But we were kidding.

SIR LENNY. So you don't think I'm observant?

SIR THEO. No. None of us do. Quite the opposite.

SIR LENNY. That's um. Ow. That stings a bit.

SIR THEO. Sorry.

SIR LENNY. So then, the forest isn't moving?

SIR THEO. Forests don't move.

SIR LENNY. Okay. Right. Of course they don't.

(*The* **MERRY MEN** *enter from the far end of the stage, holding branches, bushes, parts of trees. They begin to shoot arrows.*)

(*On the other side of the stage,* **SIR LENNY** *is hit with an arrow. He falls, seemingly from the high wall of the castle.*)

SIR LENNY. AAAARGHLLAGGGGHH!

(**SIR THEO** *watches him fall.*)

SIR THEO. Huh. Lookit that. The forest was moving. Hey you guys! I think we're under att–

(**SIR THEO** *is also hit with an arrow.*)

(*As he falls.*) –ack!

ALANNA. (*To audience, while the battle rages around her.*) We pick off all visible guards and make to scale the castle walls. It's fortunate most of the forces are searching Sherwood. I forget to worry about what face to make. I am too busy watching for arrows or falling oil. And keeping one eye always one eye on Scarlett.

26

The Tower Prison

*(**MARIAN** alone.)*

MARIAN. Guard! Guard! I need a guard.

*(Metal door opens. **GUARD 1** enters.)*

GUARD 1. What is it?

MARIAN. Oh my. I have a woman issue. Will you turn around for a moment.

GUARD 1. Should I leave?

MARIAN. No. No. Just one moment. I don't want to offend your sensibilities.

GUARD 1. Well, okay.

> *(**GUARD 1** turns around. **MARIAN** puts him in a chokehold, draws his sword. She cuts his throat [or knocks him out with the hilt], then takes his keys and opens her shackles and the big metal door. She is free!)*

27

The Prince's Chamber

> (**PRINCE JOHN** *is tying a message to a pigeon's leg. He goes to a window to throw the carrier pigeon out.*)

PRINCE JOHN. Go Florence. Go! Fly with all speed.

> (*Holding pigeon up to his ear as if she has spoken.*)

What? Yes, speed! Find your way to my men straight and true like an arrow. (*Again.*) Yes, my men. Go to the Sheriff. Or someone who can read. Be hit not with the arrows of my enemy. Go, fly! (*Again.*) Yes, that's what I said. Don't stop to fraternize with other pigeons. Fly as if your life depends on it. Because mine surely does. A pigeon. A pigeon. My kingdom for this pigeon!

> (*He throws the pigeon out the window. The pigeon may physically drop to the ground, comically, but* **PRINCE JOHN** *watches it fly into the distance.*)

> (**MARIAN** *bursts into the Prince's chamber, but now she is dressed as Robin Hood.*)

Uh-oh.

> (*Out the window.*)

Fly faster!

ROBIN. Prince John. I hear you've been looking for me.

PRINCE JOHN. Guards!! Guards!!

ROBIN. Is there any reason why I shouldn't cut off your head?

> (**ROBIN** *approaches, sword drawn.* **PRINCE JOHN** *evades.*)

PRINCE JOHN. Now, now. Let's not be too hasty. The people would rebel. The kingdom would topple.

ROBIN. I'm not so concerned with that. King Richard will return.

PRINCE JOHN. *(Laughs.)* You really think he is any different than me?

ROBIN. If he isn't, he can die after you.

PRINCE JOHN. But I am necessary! I am the king!

ROBIN. No.

> *(The **GUARDS** finally enter. At least two. **ROBIN** fights them with swords or hand to hand.)*

PRINCE JOHN. Oh good!

> *(**ROBIN** defeats one, who writhes moaning on the ground, and then goes back to fighting the other. While this is happening, **PRINCE JOHN** locates a crossbow. He "shoots" an arrow at **ROBIN**. In other words, the crossbow fires, making a "thunk" noise.)*

Ha! Not so powerful now, are you? Bullseye.

> *(**ROBIN** is turned away from the audience and when she turns back there is an arrow sticking out of her. She may hold it at the base with one hand. She stumbles but doesn't fall.)*

ROBIN. A present from the king. A wound. Not so deep as a well or wide as a church door but it'll do.

> *(**ROBIN**, pulls the arrow out, continues to fight the **GUARDS**. **MORE GUARDS** enter. **PRINCE JOHN** escapes while **ROBIN** fights. It looks as though she's done for, but then **LITTLE JOHN** and **ALANNA** enter, and with **ROBIN** they defeat the **GUARDS**.)*

Little John. Alan à Dale. How nice of you to come.

ALANNA. The prisoners have been freed.

LITTLE JOHN. We came back for you, Robin.

ALANNA. We should go.

ROBIN. I had the Prince cornered. He's here still in one room or another. In a nook. Or hiding behind a curtain.

ALANNA. Oh but you're hurt.

ROBIN. Just an arrow.

LITTLE JOHN. Are you going to be okay, Robin?

> *(Sound of trumpets. They look out the window.)*

ROBIN. The Sheriff's men coming from Sherwood.

LITTLE JOHN. Let's get you to safety.

ROBIN. The fight is not over.

ALANNA. The fight will never be over.

ROBIN. I am needed.

ALANNA. You are always needed.

LITTLE JOHN. What about Marian? Is she safe?

ROBIN. Safe enough.

> *(**ROBIN** and **LITTLE JOHN** exit and join the fray already in progress.)*

28

The Castle Grounds

(The big fight. Archers shooting arrows. Swords clashing. Most everybody is in the fight. **ROBIN** *fights wounded.* **ALANNA** *and* **WILL** *fight back to back.)*

SHERIFF. Don't let him get away this time, men! I outlaw you, outlaw.

ROBIN. Aim for the knees, Merry Men...and Much. The Sheriff's men will bow to us.

GUARD 1. *(Knocking the hat off* **WILL.***)* What's this? They're women! All the Merry Men are wo–

*(***GUARD 1** *is killed by* **WILL.***)*

WILL. No one heard nothing.

ALANNA. Robin, there are too many! We should retire to Sherwood and live to fight another day.

ROBIN. You are wise, Alan.

ALANNA. I will cover your escape.

(The **MERRY MEN** *retreat.* **ALANNA** *picks off the* **GUARDS** *with her bow. They fall. Then* **ALANNA** *follows the* **MERRY MEN.***)*

29

Sherwood Forest

(The **MERRY MEN**, *bandaging wounds, wiping blood from their swords, etc.* **ROBIN** *lies on her back, hurt.)*

LITTLE JOHN. We succeeded, Robin. The jails are empty.

ROBIN. But he will just fill them again.

ALANNA. Then we will empty them again.

ROBIN. You will have to do it without me.

LITTLE JOHN. Don't say that.

MUCH. You'll recover, Robin. You have to.

WILL. He'll be okay. Robin Hood is the strongest man that ever lived.

ROBIN. Thank you all. I appreciate it. But I'm not long for this earth. I love you all dearly. It's been an honor to fight with you.

MUCH. For us too, Robin.

*(***MERRY MEN** *ad lib agreement.)*

ROBIN. I need a minute alone with Alan.

(Other **MERRY MEN** *move away or exit.)*

ALANNA. What can I do?

ROBIN. I need you to continue to fight for the poor.

ALANNA. Of course.

ROBIN. I want you to be me.

ALANNA. I don't understand.

ROBIN. Robin Hood can never die. He is too important. He must live on to fight for those who can't fight for themselves. You must take over as Robin Hood.

ALANNA. But.

ROBIN. I've seen you fight. I've seen you shoot. I know you can do it. We need your leadership. We need Robin Hood. Will you do it?

ALANNA. How can I not?

ROBIN. Take my hat. Take my bow. Fight for good. Rob the rich.

ALANNA. Yes, Robin.

ROBIN. That's you, now.

>   (**ALANNA** *puts the hat on, does her best "Robin Hood."*)

And will you get Little John for me?

>   (**ALANNA** *exits and comes back with* **LITTLE JOHN.***)*

LITTLE JOHN. What happened to your hat, Robin? You look like, well you look like –

ROBIN. *(As* **MARIAN.***)* Marian? That's because I am Marian.

LITTLE JOHN. But – I thought – Didn't – weren't – I mean. Hold on. Oh. Hmmmm. Well that explains a lot, doesn't it?

MARIAN. There has never been anyone but you, Little John.

LITTLE JOHN. Oh, Marian. All this time.

MARIAN. I know.

LITTLE JOHN. All this time the two people I loved most in the world were one person. I feel better about our wrestling now.

MARIAN. Our time together was everything to me. I only regret not telling you sooner.

LITTLE JOHN. You're not dying. You can't.

MARIAN. Sorry, old friend.

LITTLE JOHN. What will I do without you?

MARIAN. You have to be strong, Little John.

LITTLE JOHN. I'm the strongest.

MARIAN. I know you are. Take my hand.

LITTLE JOHN. *(Taking her hand.)* You're so soft.

MARIAN. When you think of me, I hope you will think nice things.

LITTLE JOHN. How could I not?

MARIAN. I wish there was a word that means smoldering of love deferred.

LITTLE JOHN. Are you talking about me and you? Friendship? Selflessness? Love? Acorn? We could call it acorn.

MARIAN. Of course we could. *(Gasps in pain.)*

LITTLE JOHN. Does it hurt a lot?

MARIAN. Not as much as never loving you.

LITTLE JOHN. We always loved each other. I just didn't know that's what it was called.

MARIAN. Come closer.

> (**MARIAN/ROBIN** *kisses him.*)

I've been wanting to do that for a long time.

> *(Then she dies.)*

LITTLE JOHN. Me too. Robin? Me too. Robin? Marian? Nooo!

> (**LITTLE JOHN** *picks her up, if possible. He holds her and weeps.*)

I will avenge you, Robin. Marian. MarianRobin. RobinMarian. Don't worry, Robin. I will do terrible things in your name. And good things. And terrible things. For your love.

30

Sherwood Forest / The Castle

(**ALANNA** *in Sherwood and* **PRINCE JOHN** *in the castle, both at the same time.* **PRINCE JOHN** *talks to* **GUARD 2** *and the* **SHERIFF.**)

ALANNA. This is my Robin Hood face.

(**WILL** *enters, kisses* **ALANNA.**)

WILL. You look more like Robin every day.

ALANNA. Be extra careful tonight.

WILL. I'm always careful.

(*The* **MERRY MEN** *arrive.*)

ALANNA. Are we ready to raid the king's vaults!

ALL. (*Ad lib agreement.*) Yes!

LITTLE JOHN. Lead on, Robin.

ALANNA. Forward, Men!

(*The* **MERRY MEN** *exit as they sing and march.*)

MERRY MEN.

WE ARE THE MERRY MEN.

MUCH.

AND MUCH!

ALL.

WE STEAL AGAIN AND AGAIN
AND AGAIN AND AGAIN
AND AGAIN AND AGAIN
WE ARE THE MERRY MEN.

MERRY MEN.

WE ARE THE MERRY MEN.

MUCH.

AND MUCH!

ALL.

WE LAUGH AND LAUGH AND THEN
AGAIN AND AGAIN

AND AGAIN AND AGAIN
WE ARE THE MERRY MEN.

MUCH.

AND MUCH!

(*In castle,* **PRINCE JOHN** *with* **LUCY.**)

PRINCE JOHN. Richard!

(*Blackout.*)

End of Play

CPSIA information can be obtained
at www.ICGtesting.com
Printed in the USA
BVHW091815110522
636755BV00006B/819